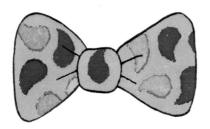

First published 1992 by Walker Books Ltd
87 Vauxhall Walk, London SE11 5HJ

This edition published 2009

2 4 6 8 10 9 7 5 3 1

© 1992 Nick Sharratt

The right of Nick Sharratt to be identified as author/illustrator of this work has been
asserted by him in accordance with the Copyright, Designs and Patents Act 1988

This book has been typeset in AT Arta

Printed in China

British Library Cataloguing in Publication Data:
a catalogue record for this book is available from the British Library.

ISBN 978-0-7445-2230-3

www.walker.co.uk

Monday Run-Day

Nick Sharratt

WALKER BOOKS

AND SUBSIDIARIES

LONDON · BOSTON · SYDNEY · AUCKLAND

Monday
run-day

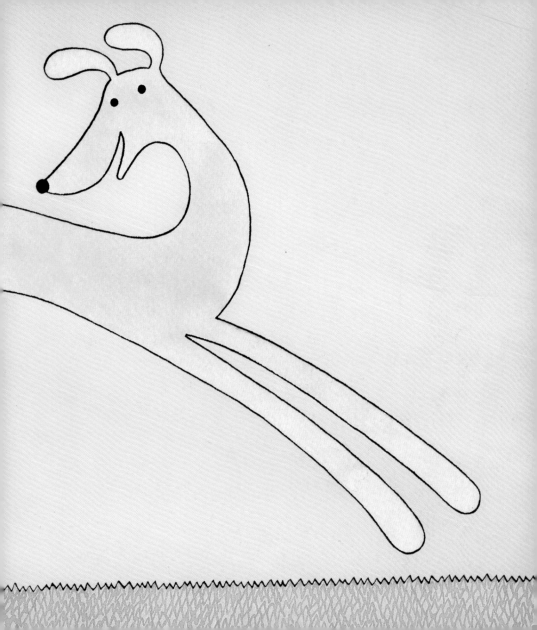

Tuesday
snooze-day

Wednesday
friends-day

Thursday
grrrs-day

Friday
tie-day

Saturday splatter-day

Sunday
bun-day

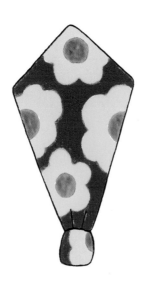